This igloo book belongs to:

....

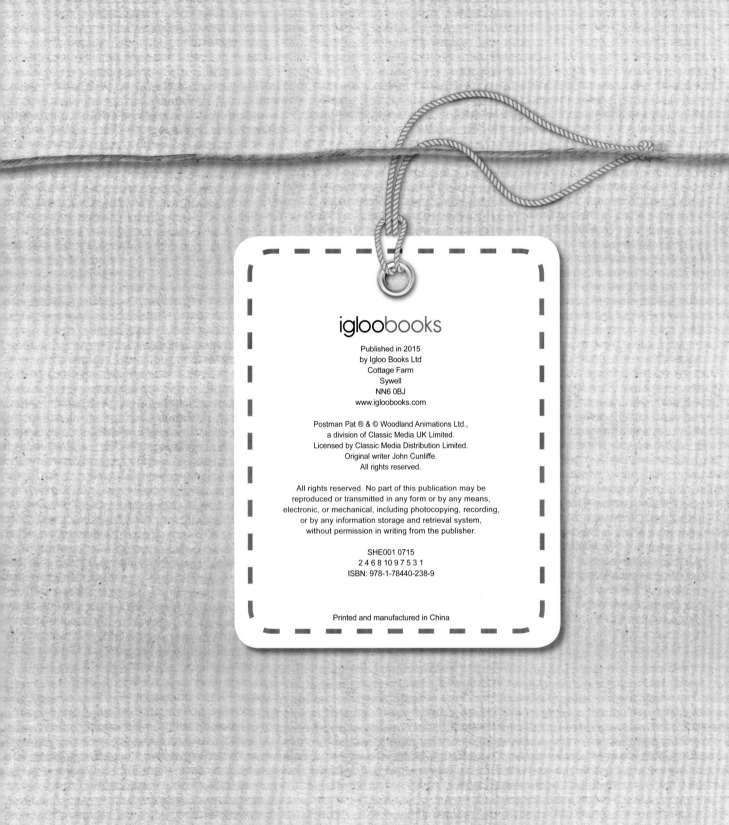

igloobooks

Published in 2015
by Igloo Books Ltd
Cottage Farm
Sywell
NN6 0BJ
www.igloobooks.com

Postman Pat ® & © Woodland Animations Ltd.,
a division of Classic Media UK Limited.
Licensed by Classic Media Distribution Limited.
Original writer John Cunliffe.
All rights reserved.

SHE001 0715
2 4 6 8 10 9 7 5 3 1
ISBN: 978-1-78440-238-9

Printed and manufactured in China

Postman Pat

Storytime Collection

CONTENTS

Postman Pat

Storytime Collection

PAT 4

igloobooks

Postman Pat

A RUNAWAY COW

Postman Pat was delivering Ted's post, when his phone rang its special ring.

"Special Delivery Service, Postman Pat speaking," he answered. There was a loud crash on the other end of the phone.

"Can you get here really quickly?" asked Ben at the mail centre. Then the phone went dead.

"Jess, it sounds like Ben needs our help!" said Postman Pat.

When Postman Pat got to the mail centre and saw the special delivery, he couldn't believe his eyes!

"Meet Daisy, your special delivery for today," announced Ben. "She's for Alf."

The cow licked Pat's face. SLURRP!

"Eugh! Thank you, Daisy. That's quite enough," said Postman Pat, edging away.

"The Special Delivery Service can deliver anything, but an animal needs proper care," said Postman Pat.

"Let's find out what vehicle you'll need," said Ben, tapping on his keyboard.

The computer showed an animal trailer.

"Amy's got a horsebox," said Postman Pat. "I'm sure she'll lend it to us."

Daisy and Jess did not seem to be making friends.

Jess meowed very loudly. The cow mooed and ran out of the mail centre.

"Come back!" called Postman Pat, but the cow was gone.

"I'll go after Daisy!" said Postman Pat. "Ben, you call Amy for help."

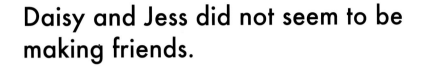

Postman Pat raced towards the market.

"Please stand back everyone, while I catch this special delivery!" Pat shouted.

No one could persuade the cow to move, but Pat had an idea.

He tried his best to slip a rope around Daisy's neck, but she ran off, pulling him behind her! Postman Pat couldn't hold on for long, and Daisy charged off out of the town.

"Stop!" called Pat, jumping into his van.

Amy was driving along when she met Daisy in the lane.

"I think I've found your special delivery," laughed Amy, as Postman Pat drove up.

With a lot of kicking and fussing and mooing, Daisy went into the horsebox.

"Special Delivery Service underway!" cheered a muddy Postman Pat.

Just as she was driving off, Amy heard a strange noise coming from inside the horsebox.

"That sounds like Jess," said Amy. "He must have got shut in the horsebox with Daisy."

Postman Pat let Jess out and gave him a cuddle but, while they weren't looking, Daisy strolled out and walked away up the cliff path!

Alf drove up on his tractor.

"Alf! Just the man," called Postman Pat.
"I've got a special delivery for you.
It's a new cow."

"I can see that," said Alf.
"What on earth is she
doing on that cliff?"

Pat looked up in surprise.
Poor Daisy was stuck and
mooed helplessly.

"This is a job for the Special Delivery Service helicopter!" said Postman Pat. "I'll need Amy's help, too."

Postman Pat and Amy rushed back to the mail centre to get the helicopter and the other equipment they needed.

"Operation Rescue Daisy is underway!" said Postman Pat, as he took off with Amy hooked on to the winch.

Daisy was very scared by the noise of the helicopter.

"We'd better hurry, Pat," Amy said into her headset.

Postman Pat got the helicopter in position and carefully lowered Amy. She put the harness around Daisy and they were both gently lifted off the ground.

"One special delivery on its way!" said Postman Pat and he lifted her safely towards Alf's farm.

No one could believe their eyes when they saw Amy and the flying cow!

Soon they were all safely on the ground in Alf's field.

"Thank you, Amy and Pat," said Alf. "You saved Daisy!"

"All in a day's work for the Special Delivery Service!" said Postman Pat, as Daisy gave him a big, wet kiss. "Mission accomplished!"

MISSION ACCOMPLISHED

POSTMAN PAT®

A BOUNCY DELIVERY

Postman Pat was delivering a large parcel to Michael at the shop.

"Oh no! They've sent me too many!" said Michael, as boxes of plasters tumbled out all over the floor.

Just then, Pat's phone rang its special ring.

"Special Delivery Service, Postman Pat speaking," he answered.

"You need to come quickly," said Ben's voice. "I've got an urgent parcel for delivery."

When Postman Pat arrived at the mail centre, Ben showed him the parcel that needed a special delivery.

"There's no label on it, Pat," said Ben. "I don't know who it's for."

Suddenly, the parcel started squeaking and wriggling around. Jess jumped up in surprise.

"Look out!" shouted Postman Pat, as the parcel started to grow!

The parcel grew bigger and bigger until finally, it stopped squeaking and burst into a giant bouncy castle!

It was so big that it squished Postman Pat, Ben and Jess up against the wall.

"I wonder who it could be for?" said Pat.

Ben's computer told him that the castle was for the school.

"This is certainly the biggest special delivery challenge I've ever had," said Postman Pat. "Let's get the air out to make it easier."

Postman Pat looked, but couldn't find the air valve and no matter how hard they tried to push, or squash, or even run at the castle, they just bounced off it again!

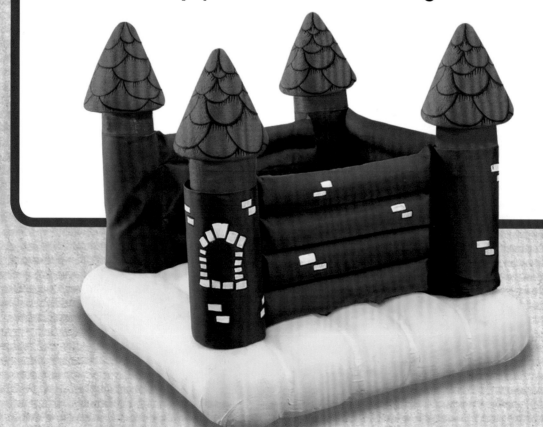

Just then, PC Selby arrived.
"Need some help, Pat?" he asked.

The three friends tried and tried,
but they couldn't deflate the
bouncy castle.

"I know what to do!"
cried Postman Pat.
"This is a job for the
Special Delivery
Service helicopter!
Come on, Jess!"

Pat took off in the Special Delivery helicopter, with Jess by his side, and they lifted the bouncy castle out of the mail centre.

"Now, we must be careful," said Pat to Jess. "We have never had a special delivery like this before."

At the mail centre, Ben and PC Selby watched as Postman Pat took off with the bouncy castle.

"Let's hope that the bouncy castle gets there in one piece," said PC Selby. "The children will be so disappointed if it's broken."

"Don't worry, PC Selby," said Ben, "We can always count on Pat to make the delivery on time."

The children couldn't believe their eyes when they saw a helicopter flying towards their school.

"What's that?" gasped Julian.

"It's our bouncy castle!" cried Lizzie.

"Special delivery, for Mrs Taylor!" Postman Pat shouted down.

"Just in time," said Lauren. "Postman Pat has saved the day!"

Postman Pat lowered the castle to the ground and landed his helicopter in a nearby field.

Suddenly, there was a loud hissing noise coming from the bouncy castle. Jess was bouncing up and down on it and his sharp claws were making holes everywhere!

"Meow," said Jess sadly, looking at the deflated castle.

"What are we going to do now?" asked Meera, sadly.

"We'll need something to cover all of these holes," said Ted.

Suddenly, Postman Pat had a good idea. He raced over to Michael's shop.

"I need all of those plasters," announced Postman Pat.

"All of them?" gasped Michael in surprise.

The children helped Postman Pat stick plasters over the holes.

"Well done, Pat! It looks like it's fixed," said Lauren. "How are we going to blow it up again?"

"I've found the air valve!" called Lizzie.

"Ah! Can we borrow your leaf blower, Ted?" asked Postman Pat.

"Pleased to help," replied Ted.

The bouncy castle was blown up again in no time. The children couldn't wait to jump on it. Even Jess was allowed to play, with Julian holding him in his arms as he bounced.

"Thank you, Pat!" laughed the children, as they jumped up and down.

"No problem!" replied Postman Pat. "Special Delivery Service – mission accomplished!"

Postman pat®

A SECRET DELIVERY

It was a sunny day in Pencaster, as Postman Pat arrived at the mail centre.

Ben, the general manager, waved Postman Pat over to the office.

"Ooh, what have you got there?" asked Postman Pat.

"Ssshh!" said Ben. "This special delivery is top secret, Pat."

Ben brought out a beautiful tepee.

"Lauren has organised a treasure hunt for the children," said Ben. "The tepee is for a surprise sleepover at the end."

"The children will love that," said Pat. "Where am I taking it?"

Ben handed the directions to Pat.

"You must keep the location a secret," he said.

"You can trust us," Pat smiled, but as Jess jumped up to see the tepee, he knocked the directions into the paper shredder.

Over at the town square, Reverend Timms had gathered the children together.

"Welcome to the treasure hunt," he said. "Are you ready for your first clue?"

"Yes! Yes!" the children chorused, excitedly.

Reverend Timms held up a picture of a light bulb. The children all started whispering and ran off to solve the clue.

Meanwhile, Postman Pat was having trouble finding out where he should take the tepee.

Lauren was waiting at the secret location but, when Pat tried to ring her mobile phone, he couldn't get through to her.

"I'll have to do the treasure hunt on my own," said Postman Pat. "The clues will lead me to Lauren."

Postman Pat loaded the tepee into the van and sped off to find the first clue.

Reverend Timms was very surprised to see Postman Pat on the treasure hunt.

"I need to deliver the prize to the end, but I don't know where the finish is," explained Postman Pat.

Reverend Timms showed Postman Pat the light bulb clue.

"Hmm… street lamps, shop lights, traffic lights…" said Pat. Then, he had a thought. "The lighthouse!"

When Postman Pat arrived at the lighthouse, Bill Thompson and Lucy Selby were already there looking at the clue.

"I can't reach it," Bill said, jumping up.

The second clue was stuck on the lighthouse. It was a picture of a carrot.

"Michael sells carrots," Bill said. "Let's go!"

"Bill! Wait!" cried Postman Pat, but Bill had already disappeared.

By the time Postman Pat arrived at Michael's shop, the children had already seen the next clue and left.

"You're a bit old for a treasure hunt, Pat," smiled Michael.

"It's a long story!" replied Postman Pat.

The third clue was a picture of a rocket.

"The Greendale Rocket!" said Postman Pat. "The clue must be at the station."

Postman Pat and Jess sped over to Pencaster Station. Ajay had stuck a huge picture of a woolly sheep on the side of the train.

"There's one place I know to find sheep," Pat said. "Thompson Ground! Bye, Ajay!"

Postman Pat raced over to Thompson Ground, but he got slowed down by some sheep on the way.

"Is this what your looking for?" asked Alf, and he handed the final clue to Pat. It was a picture of a sail.

"The Jetty!" cried Pat. "Thanks Alf!" he shouted, as he jumped into the delivery van with Jess.

Over at the jetty, Ted Glenn was taking the children to the secret location by boat.

"All aboard now," Ted said. "The prize is on the island."

"I wish my dad could see me," said Julian, but Postman Pat was nowhere in sight.

Postman Pat finally arrived at the jetty, but the children were already sailing across the lake.

"We've missed the boat!" cried Postman Pat.

Then, Jess jumped into an old rowing boat in the water. Using the tepee as a sail, they quickly sailed off towards the island.

The children all waved in surprise as Pat and Jess went sailing by.

Postman Pat finally reached the island and found Amy and Lauren.

"We made it!" he said, happily.

Postman Pat quickly put up the tepee, just as the children ran onto the island. They all cheered when they saw the prize tepee.

"You missed an amazing treasure hunt, Dad," said Julian.

"Why don't you tell me all about it?" said Postman Pat. "Special Delivery Service – mission accomplished!"

Postman pat

A PRECIOUS DELIVERY

Postman Pat and Jess were having a quiet day when suddenly, Postman Pat's phone rang its special ring.

"Special Delivery Service, Postman Pat speaking," he answered.

It was Ben, at the mail centre, calling to tell Pat there was a package for immediate delivery.

Postman Pat jumped into the van with Jess.

When Postman Pat got to Pencaster, it was market day and PC Selby had closed the entire road.

"You'll have to park here and walk I'm afraid, Pat," he called.

Postman Pat was in a rush and he didn't have time for that. He borrowed a bicycle and jumped onto it. He whizzed off at high speed, with Jess sitting in the basket.

At the mail centre, Ben showed Postman Pat the special delivery.

"These are duck eggs," Ben explained. "Greendale pond is going to have six baby ducklings. You must get them to Amy quickly. She will keep them warm until they hatch."

"That really is a special delivery," said Postman Pat. "We'd better get going, Jess!"

As Postman Pat was carrying the precious eggs back to his van, he met Mrs Goggins and her dog, Bonnie.

Bonnie leapt up at Jess and chased him through the market.

"Don't worry, Jess," he said. "Bonnie is only playing with you."

Postman Pat put the eggs down on the stall while he crawled underneath to rescue a worried looking Jess.

When Postman Pat stood up again, the eggs had disappeared.

"I'm afraid Michael just bought them for his shop," explained Dorothy. "I didn't know they were special. They looked just like all the others."

"Oh, dear," said Postman Pat. "Come on, Jess. We might catch him if we hurry!"

In the village, Sara was out doing some food shopping.

"Hello, Michael," she said. "Nisha and I are making cakes. I need sugar, butter... eggs."

Sara put the precious eggs in her basket and waved goodbye to Michael.

After Sara left, Postman Pat arrived at Michael's shop.

"Have you got the eggs you bought from Dorothy?" asked Postman Pat.

"Sorry, Pat," replied Michael. "I've just sold them to Sarah."

"I have to get over there right now," said Postman Pat, as he raced back to his van.

As Postman Pat made his way over to Sara's, his van made a coughing and spluttering noise.

"Oh, no!" cried Pat, as the van slowly came to a halt.

Luckily, Pumpkin was in a nearby field. Postman Pat hopped onto his back.

"Quickly Pumpkin!" cried Pat. "We must get to those eggs!"

At the café, Sara, Nisha and the children were making cakes.

First, they weighed the sugar. Then, they mixed in the butter and the big bag of flour.

"Now for the eggs," said Sara.

She picked up an egg and was just about to crack it when...

"No-o-o-o-o-o-o-o!" shouted Postman Pat, bursting through the front door.

"Those aren't just ordinary eggs! I have to get them to Amy so she can hatch them."

At that moment, the eggs started to wobble and crack.

"We haven't got much time," said Pat. "Jess can keep them warm until we can get there."

"Have you got the eggs?" asked Amy, as Postman Pat drove up.

"I'm afraid not," he replied. "I've got something even better than that."

Jess jumped out of the van, followed, by six baby ducks.

"They've hatched!" cried Amy. "Look, they think Jess is their mummy."

"Special Delivery Service – mission accomplished!" laughed Postman Pat.

Postman Pat

A CHILLY DELIVERY

It was the day of the Greendale Summer Festival and everyone was very excited.

"Hurray! It's going to be the best festival ever," cried Julian, happily. "Michael Lam is organising it and I love Chinese food!"

Suddenly, Postman Pat's phone rang its special ring. It was Ben at the mail centre, with an urgent special delivery for Pat.

Postman Pat and Jess were very surprised when they got to the mail centre and saw the special delivery.

"It's a huge block of ice," explained Ben. "It's got to be delivered to Greendale by 12 o'clock, in time for the festival."

"I wonder what the ice can be for?" said Postman Pat, loading it into his van with the forklift truck.

At the café, Michael, Nisha and Sara were busy cooking.

"Right, we've got less than an hour to prepare the best Chinese banquet that Greendale has ever tasted," cried Michael.

They chopped, fried and baked until all the food was ready.

"Well done, team!" cheered Michael, happily. "Now we just need my surprise special delivery to add the final glorious touch to our creation."

Back at the mail centre, Postman Pat was ready to go.

"Okay, Pat! You're all set," Ben said. "See you at the festival."

"Greendale here we come!" cried Postman Pat, as Jess jumped in beside him.

Just then, Ben noticed something.

"Oh no, the door isn't shut properly! Pat!" Ben shouted, but it was too late. Pat and Jess had gone.

Ben called PC Selby.

"Pat's in trouble!" he cried.

"A huge block of ice and the back doors aren't shut," said PC Selby. "That could be very dangerous. Where is he?"

Ben checked his computer. It told him the van was on its way back towards Greendale.

"Leave it to me, Ben!" said PC Selby and he set off in his police car with the siren screaming.

Postman Pat was driving along, humming to himself. He didn't realise that the van's door was open.

As the van went round a corner, Pat heard a big BANG!

"Miaow!" wailed Jess.

"What happened?" asked Pat.

He stopped the van quickly. The ice had fallen out and slid into a field full of sheep!

At the festival, everyone was busy getting things prepared and ready.

"Any sign of my special delivery yet?" asked Michael, arriving with the delicious food.

"Not yet," replied Lauren. "Are you going to tell us what it is, Michael?"

"All right! My special delivery is..."

The children waited patiently with bated breath.

"A surprise!" announced Michael, and everyone laughed loudly.

Back in the field, the sheep were very curious about the ice.

"We need to get this back in the van," said Postman Pat. "It's already starting to melt away."

Postman Pat tried to move the ice, but it was too heavy.

Just then, PC Selby arrived in his police car. Alf was close behind on his tractor.

"Ben thought you might need some help," said PC Selby.

Jess herded the sheep out of the way and Alf pushed the ice with his tractor. Soon, the ice was safely back in the van.

"We've got five minutes to get to the festival!" cried Postman Pat.

"You'll never make it!" said PC Selby.

Then they had an idea. PC Selby led the way, with his siren howling, and Postman Pat, Jess and Alf followed closely behind.

At the village green, Michael was looking worried.

Just then, he heard the sound of a loud siren.

PC Selby's police car came quickly rushing round the corner followed by Pat's van and Alf's tractor.

The villagers cheered as Postman Pat announced: "A special delivery for Michael Lam!"

Everyone gathered around to look at the surprise, but Michael's face dropped.

"A big ice cube? That's not what I ordered," he said. "I ordered an ice sculpture of a dragon!"

There was an awkward pause, then Jess jumped on top of Ted's toolbox.

"Jess, you're a genius!" said Postman Pat. "Don't worry, Michael. You've ordered a special delivery ice sculpture and that's exactly what you'll get."

The sound of hammering and banging came from inside the van.

"It's finished!" Postman Pat cried, revealing an ice sculpture of Jess.

Michael was open-mouthed. "It's great, Pat!" he exclaimed. "Better than a dragon. Let the summer festival begin!"

Everyone cheered and rushed for the food!

Postman Pat smiled. "Special Delivery Service – mission accomplished," he said.

postman pat®

A MUSICAL DELIVERY

The Special Delivery Service van was being cleaned at Ted's car wash. Bubbles were everywhere!

Suddenly, Postman Pat's phone rang its special ring.

"Special Delivery Service, Postman Pat speaking," he answered. It was Ben, at the mail centre.

"Pat, I've got an urgent special delivery for you," said Ben. "It's over at Pencaster Station with Ajay."

Postman Pat arrived at Pencaster Station and found Ajay playing a piano.

Postman Pat's phone rang again. It was Ben. He said that the piano had to be delivered to the school in time for Lizzy to play her first piano solo in a concert.

Ajay helped Postman Pat push the piano into the van.

"Come on, Jess," said Pat. "Lizzy is waiting for us."

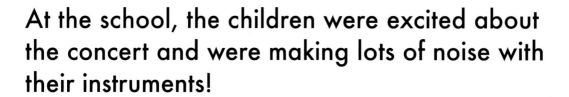

At the school, the children were excited about the concert and were making lots of noise with their instruments!

Julian played the drums and Bill played a guitar. Lizzy practised on an electric keyboard.

"Good news, Lizzy," said Lauren.
"The piano is on its way. You'll have plenty of
time to rehearse before the concert starts."

As Postman Pat and Jess raced to the school, some cows wandered into the middle of the road! Pat braked and the van screeched to a halt. He jumped out of the van. Stopping so quickly had made one of the van's tyres go flat.

"It's a puncture Jess, we need some help," said Postman Pat.

He called Ted at the garage.

Ted soon arrived, but he hadn't brought the tool he needed to change the tyre. So, they decided to drive the piano to the school in the back of Ted's van. Ted went to get the piano out of Postman Pat's van.

"Nice and steady now, Ted," said Postman Pat. "Not too fast."

Suddenly, the piano slid out of the van, with Ted on top of it!

"Whooah!" called out Ted. "Oh dear!"

Postman Pat and Jess jumped out of the way as Ted and the piano rolled past them. It smashed through a gate, with Ted still holding on tightly!

"Oh! Who'd have thought a piano could go so fast!" shouted Ted.

At last the piano slowed down and stopped in the middle of a muddy field. Ted climbed safely down, but then he fell backwards into a dirty puddle.

"Are you all right, Ted?" asked Postman Pat. "We need to get this piano into your truck."

"It's too muddy, Pat," said Ted. "We'll never push it out of this field."

Just then, Jess meowed and leapt on to a trolley on the nearby train track.

"The trolley!" laughed Pat. "Jess, you clever cat. This disused track goes all the way to Greendale. We could use the trolley to get us there."

Postman Pat and Ted carefully strapped the piano on to the trolley.

Then, they took turns to push down on the trolley's lever. They started to move slowly along the track.

"Heave ho, heave ho!" Postman Pat and Ted called out, as they pushed the lever.

"Faster, Ted, I've got to get this special delivery to the school, or the show can't go on!" puffed Postman Pat.

At last, the trolley and the piano arrived at Greendale Station. Postman Pat and Ted huffed and puffed as they took the piano off the trolley.

Just then, Pumpkin clip-clopped past with Amy.

Pat had a great idea. Amy carefully tied a harness around Pumpkin, so he could pull the piano along behind him.

"Come on Pumpkin, that's it," said Amy, happily.
"One piano on its way!"

Lizzy was waiting outside the school with all her friends. Finally, they spotted Postman Pat with the piano.

"I haven't had time to practise," said Lizzy sadly. "What if I make a mistake?"

"No one will mind if you make a mistake, Lizzy," said Postman Pat.

"Everyone just wants to hear you play the piano!" cheered on Meera.

At last, the concert began. Lizzy nervously began to play. Soon, she was playing a wonderful tune on the piano.

The audience clapped, and everyone shouted "Hooray!"

"Thanks, Pat," said Lizzy.

"You're welcome," said Postman Pat. "The Special Delivery Service always gets through. Mission accomplished!"

WELL DONE!
MISSION ACCOMPLISHED!